NO BRAINER

NO BRAINER

LEA BEDDIA

ORCA BOOK PUBLISHERS

Published in Canada and the United States in 2026 by Orca Book Publishers.

Library and Archives Canada Cataloguing in Publication
Title: No brainer / Lea Beddia.
Names: Beddia, Lea, author.
Series: Orca anchor.
Description: Series statement: Orca anchor
Identifiers: Canadiana (print) 20250141485 |
Canadiana (ebook) 20250147270 | ISBN 9781459841963 (softcover) |
ISBN 9781459841970 (PDF) | ISBN 9781459841987 (EPUB)
Subjects: LCGFT: Novels. | LCGFT: High interest-low vocabulary books.
Classification: LCC PS8603.E4245 N6 2026 | DDC jC813/.6—dc23

Library of Congress Control Number: 2025932573

Summary: In this high-interest accessible novel for teen readers, Liv finds herself at the center of a feminist movement when she's teased and reprimanded for not wearing a bra.

Orca Book Publishers is committed to reducing the consumption of nonrenewable resources in the production of our books. We make every effort to use materials that support a sustainable future.

Orca Book Publishers gratefully acknowledges the support for its publishing programs provided by the following agencies: the Government of Canada, the Canada Council for the Arts and the Province of British Columbia through the BC Arts Council and the Book Publishing Tax Credit.

Cover artwork by IrishaDesign/Shutterstock.com.
Design by Ella Collier.
Edited by Gabrielle Prendergast.
Author photo by Sarah Fortin Photographe.

Printed and bound in Canada.

29 28 27 26 • 1 2 3 4

CERTIFIED CANADIAN PUBLISHER

ORCA BOOK PUBLISHERS
orcabook.com

To girls

Chapter One

"I can't squeeze into these," I say. The jeans Mia chose for me don't make it past my knees. I pry them off and drape them over the door. "Buttons, zippers, no thanks." I pull my joggers back on and exit the dressing room. "Ah, comfort." I let out a sigh.

"You can't live in those pants forever," Mia says.

"I disagree. See?" I twirl and bow. "This is me. Living." I slap my legs. "In these pants!"

"We can find some *new* comfy jeans. Stretch denim," Mia says.

"My joggers are perfect." I look Mia up and down. White V-neck T-shirt. Slim jeans. She's got narrow hips and little boobs. Plus she's comfy in anything.

"It's fun to have new stuff," she says.

"If it fits," I say. She's the one who loves to shop. I would rather binge Netflix, but I'd also rather be with her than alone. Mia and her family were away on a one-month cruise at the end of the summer, so I'm making up for lost Mia time.

"I'm sure the jeans look good on you," Mia says.

"They're too tight. I couldn't even bend my knees, like Frankenstein. They didn't feel good, so they're a no."

Now it's Mia's turn to look at me. She thinks for a second. "New tracksuits?" she asks.

"I have plenty. I'm done shopping."

"How about some pretty panties?" she says, smiling.

"What?" My face heats up. "Why don't you say that a little louder?" I whisper. "I don't think they heard the word *panties* in the parking lot." I hang the jeans back on the rack.

Mia helps with the ten other pairs I'll never wear. "*Panties* is not a bad word," she says. "And you need something to make you feel pretty under all that jogging material."

"Joggers are built for fun." I check myself out in the mirror. My bulky pink top comes just below my chest, showing off a little tummy. I pull the drawstring on my pants to cinch my waist, accentuating my hips. "And I do feel pretty. Who needs sexy undies? It's a waste of money." I keep my voice low. No need for the sales lady to hear me. "I mean, who's going to see them? My Hello Kitty stuffies?"

"No. Not for *that.*" Mia starts laughing. She crosses her legs and holds on to a clothing rack. It's her *I gotta stop what I'm doing or I'll pee my pants* laugh. When she can breathe, she says, "Just...to feel good. Underneath. You know?"

"I do feel good. Everywhere." I rotate my hips, and she's in ultra giggle mode again. "But I don't want to stuff all this into jeans. If people want to look at my butt, they can look at it in sweats."

"Who do you want looking at your butt?" Mia asks.

"No one," I say. "And I'd rather put my energy into cramming for math than cramming myself into tight clothes."

"Mmm, math is so sexy," Mia says, rolling her eyes. "How about new bras? You can always use those."

"Sure, because after stuffing my butt into tight jeans, you want me to crush my boobs into a bra? My body needs to breathe. Why do you love shopping so much?" I ask.

"Your mom gave you cash. She told me you could spend it all. It is my duty now to make sure you do."

"Fine." The truth is, even if we are shopping and talking about butts and bras, being with

Mia feels right. Like a cozy pair of joggers. We've been friends for so long, we just fit.

Mia walks into the underwear section and chooses three bras with pretty lace. I have never put on anything so fancy. "These bras are fun. Try them," Mia says, and hands them to me.

"Fine," I say again.

In the changing room, I try on one of the flimsy bras she found. The wire cuts into my ribs. The straps pull at my skin. I try to clasp the back three times. I can't get it hooked. Off it goes. I toss it over the door. "No way," I say. I pull on my top, then walk out.

"Too much lace?" Mia asks.

"Not enough," I say. "Not to cover these

beauties." I make a gesture around my chest to display my gifts.

"Show-off," Mia says.

"They're just boobs," I tell her, twirling the lacy bra around my index finger. "This thing is not strong enough for me," I add.

"Might be the wrong size," Mia says, looking at the tag. "It's a C cup."

"Maybe when I was twelve. Definitely not anymore." I pull the bra like a slingshot, hoping to hit Mia in the chest, but I aim too high and it pops into the air. It rises in a perfect arc and lands on the cash register. The woman behind the counter jumps. She glares at us. Mia grabs my hand and we bolt out of the store, bursting with giggles.

We escape into the mall. "We'll never be allowed in there again," Mia says. "Where to next? No more helicopter bras—I promise."

"No lace either," I say. "I'm done with shopping for today. Mom didn't say what to spend the money on."

"What do you have in mind?" Mia asks.

"I'm starving," I say, thinking of my favorite bakery. "Let's go to Sugar Buns."

"That should be your nickname," Mia says, giving me a friendly slap on my behind.

"Shut up!" I chase her all the way to the food court.

Chapter Two

The first day of school has a precise smell. Cool air of a crisp late summer morning. Something cooking in the cafeteria mixed with whatever they use to buff the floors. I walk to the changing room for first period and get into my gym sweats. I wait in the gym, where the volleyball nets are up. Not an original choice, since Ms. Myers, the PE teacher, is the girls' volleyball coach. A group of boys are shirtless, already working up a sweat.

One boy, Enrico, is dribbling the ball between his legs, moving away from a buddy who's trying to grab the ball away. Enrico's back is sweaty. He has smooth dark skin. His arms do that thing where you can see the muscles tighten under the skin. He's fit and fast. I can't lie and say he doesn't look good running around shirtless, but it's his feet I can't stop looking at. Light and fast as heck, but graceful too. When his friend finally gets the ball from Enrico, the boy runs with it and cheers, then pretends to throw it in Enrico's face. Girls would never get away with playing this way. And I can't imagine what would happen if we played shirtless.

I haven't even started moving yet, but my cheeks are hot suddenly. From looking at

Enrico? From thinking about being shirtless? I rub my face and try to think of something else. Mia arrives a few minutes later, thank goodness. Who wants to go through the first day of school without their bestie?

"PE first period. Someone hates us," Mia says.

"I don't think anyone cares enough to hate us," I point out.

"This still sucks," Mia says. She eyes the shirtless boys. "Or maybe not."

Now they're trying to impress each other by dunking the volleyball into the basketball nets. They're loud, squeaking their sneakers on the waxed floor on purpose. I hate that sound. "So shallow," I say. I tease Mia with a jab in the shoulder.

The boys spin the balls on their fingers and yell anytime someone drops one. Enrico's friend Jerry is the loudest.

Ms. Myers blows her whistle, and everyone stops what they're doing. "Enough fooling around," she yells. "Shirts on. And pick up the balls," she tells the boys.

"Yeah, pick up your balls," Jerry says, mocking Enrico.

"Enough," Ms. Myers yells out to them again. They settle down.

She reviews the rules for volleyball, but everyone knows them by heart. First term in PE has been volleyball since seventh grade. This is our fourth time hearing the rules.

The teacher splits us into teams. Mia and I are on opposite teams, but she swaps with another girl. Ms. Myers doesn't notice. I'm with Mia, Jerry, Enrico and some of the girls from the volleyball team.

We're in position, and Enrico hands me the ball. "Your serve," he says. He's grown about a foot over the summer. His curly hair bounces as he moves. His brown skin is already shiny with sweat from running around with his friends. I am suddenly aware that I am also sweating. A lot.

I grab the ball and get ready for a serve. I fling the ball into the net.

"Try tossing it a little higher, Liv," Ms. Myers calls out. "Even if you have to jump."

"Good call, Coach," Jerry says. "Let's see you jump, Liv." But his comment throws me off, and I miss again. Enrico says something I can't hear to Jerry, who laughs.

"You got this, Liv," Mia calls.

I try again, but this time I drop the ball, and it rolls to one of the volleyball girls. She picks it up. "Maybe cup it as you hold it, before serving." The friendly girl shows me what she means.

"*Cup* the ball, Liv. You know, so it doesn't go flopping all over the place," another girl says. She has a high curly ponytail that swishes when she talks. This gets Jerry laughing again. *So dumb.*

The girl who gave me the pointer turns to her friend and Jerry. "Get over it, you two. Real mature."

"What's your problem?" I ask Ponytail Girl.

"Nothing, just trying to give you a little *support*," she says. She emphasizes the last word.

"Just serve already," Jerry says impatiently. "Or I'll do it."

"She can handle it," the friendly girl says. "You got this?"

"Got it," I say. I get into position one last time.

Jerry turns back to face me. "Maybe if you could see over your own volleyballs, you wouldn't miss the serve," he says as I wind up. I miss again, only this time I don't hit the net. I hit Jerry. He's on his knees.

"You did that on purpose," he says, cupping his private parts.

Enrico has a hand on his shoulder. “You okay, man?” Enrico asks.

Jerry whines in pain.

“Did you do that on purpose?” Mia asks.

“I wish my aim was that good,” I say. Ponytail Girl laughs. But I feel bad for saying it.

“What happened?” Ms. Myers asks.

“Accidental serve, Coach,” Enrico tells her.

“Accidental...my...balls,” Jerry growls.

“I didn’t mean to,” I say. “I’m really bad at volleyball.”

Jerry finally stands up. “She’s a danger,” he says. “Maybe if you weren’t...you know... sagging all over the place.”

I take a quick step forward, fists ready, but I don’t have the guts to punch him. Even if he deserves it.

"That's enough. Liv, Jerry, take a break," Ms. Myers says.

I'm benched, which sucks. I don't love PE, but I'll never improve if I don't get to play.

Jerry ices his testicles. The look on Enrico's face and his smile at Jerry on the bench tell me he knows Jerry is fine. After a minute the ice pack is on the bench, and Jerry is scrolling his phone. He'll be okay. He'll still be able to have children. *Yay.*

Class is almost over, and Ms. Myers is talking to Jerry across the gym. Then she comes to me. "See me after class," she says.

Perfect.

Chapter Three

Ms. Myers's office is a closet with sports gear packed in every corner.

"How's it going, Liv?" She points to the chair in front of her desk. I sit across from her.

"Other than hitting a boy in the testicles and sitting out? Good. You?"

"I get that it was an accident. The other students agree."

"I really am sorry. It wasn't fun to see him in pain or to know it was my fault."

"What happened?" Ms. Myers asks.

"I dropped the ball. I know you're always saying, 'Eyes on the ball.' I'm a little rusty. Sorry," I say.

"We're lucky he wasn't hurt worse than he was."

"Right. I said I'm sorry to him." *Wait, did I? Crap. I guess I'll have to.*

Ms. Myers turns in her chair. She unfolds and folds a hockey jersey.

"Is there anything else, Ms. Myers?" I ask.

"Some of the boys, Jerry included, felt... distracted during the game," she says.

"I shouldn't have served first. One of your volleyball girls should have gotten us started. Next time." I stand to leave.

"Wait. That's not all. What I mean is, you were distracting them."

"Got it. I'll practice my serve. Can I go? I'll be late for my next class," I say.

"I'll write you a pass." She moves around some hockey pucks. One rolls to the floor by my foot, and I hand it to her. "The thing is, some found it distracting...the way you're dressed."

I look down at my large sweatshirt. I pull at it. "This?" I ask.

"Mostly...the fact that you're clearly not... wearing a bra." She turns away from me to fold another jersey.

I feel like a soda with all the fizz gone flat. "Seriously? But I'm all covered up."

"I know, but I think...forgive me, but you may have had a growth spurt over the summer."

I think of the C-cup bra Mia had me try on. How it would have fit at the end of last year. Maybe. I've lost track.

"My clothes fit the dress code."

"I know."

"So my boobs are the distraction?" I sit up tall. "One of your volleyball girls was focused enough to help me with my serve. Maybe the boys are the problem."

"Right. Well, maybe you might be more comfortable with more support. For sports," Ms. Myers says.

"I'm comfortable, Ms. Myers. And I'm not

super into sports. I only play in gym class."

"Some students think you were...slowed down by your..." She can't even say it. She knows how stupid this is. "There are plenty of sports bras that offer support."

"Sports bras are worse than regular bras. They squeeze everything together into one sweaty uniboob," I say.

"Some tank tops have support built in. You'd have to wear something over it, of course, not to violate—"

"The dress code. Yeah, I've been to the principal's office enough times. I've got it covered. Literally. Sorry, Ms. Myers, but those clothes make it hard to move and breathe," I say.

"It's just that when you jump, or run, they... get in the way," she says.

I stand up. I hate feeling like I'm losing an argument. "They're not in my way, Ms. Myers. They are my body." I think of Mia in her tight gym T-shirt and shorts. "Would I be here if I had small boobs?"

"Your size is not the issue, Liv," Ms. Myers says.

"But it is. If I were less curvy, there'd be no problem. If anyone was distracted by my body today, I can't fix that. If Jerry is afraid to get hit again, maybe he's the one who should be wearing support. I'm not changing a thing."

Ms. Myers turns to me. "I know that, but—"

"The boys train topless all the time. Maybe we don't want to be staring at their sweaty chests. If a girl complains, she's being dramatic. Maybe the bare chests distract some of the other boys too. But they wouldn't dare say so. We know what they would be called if they did. It's not fair, Ms. Myers."

She takes her time before answering me. "You're right, Liv. I didn't mean to shame you. Jerry felt his injury was due to his distraction. I had to at least talk to you about it. But you're right. It's his issue, not yours," she says.

"Thank you, Ms. Myers," I say.

She hands me a late pass. I think that's the end of it. Until I get to math class and the only free seat is next to Jerry.

Chapter Four

I think Jerry will make a stupid comment, but he's quiet. Maybe he's too pissed about gym. He works at his pretest without a word. Pretests are as sure in math as volleyball is in PE class.

Jerry isn't finding it easy, either. He has his head in his hands, and he's banging on his calculator. I don't know why I look over at him. Maybe to make sure he's hating this as much as I am. He notices.

"What?" he says.

"I'm sorry. About before. Are you okay?"

"Yeah. Whatever," he says.

He gives me the up-and-down look that is so repulsive. I turn my back to him and finish my test. When the bell rings, he walks out before me.

On the bus I tell Mia what Ms. Myers said about wearing a bra. She can't believe it.

"So you don't agree with her?" I ask.

"No way. Why would I agree?" She offers me a bite of her granola bar. I'm not hungry.

"You were so into bra shopping," I say.

"For fun. Not because I think you have to wear one."

"Thanks," I say.

"Ms. Myers agreed with you in the end?" Mia asks.

"Yeah."

"Good. So it's over," Mia says.

"I hope so."

The next day in PE, we're split into teams again. This time Ms. Myers makes sure Jerry is not near my serve. The kind volleyball girl from yesterday, Aria, takes the first serve. Thank goodness. It goes over the net easily. The other team taps it three times and sends it over. Enrico bumps it to Ponytail Girl, who bumps it to me, and I send it over the net. No problem. When it's back to us, we gain a point on Ponytail's spike.

It's a smooth game until we rotate. Now I'm standing in front of the net, facing Jerry. He gives me the up-and-down look again. I let it bother me for a second until we're playing again. A boy from the other team sends the ball over the net, right at me. I gear up for a spike. Jerry tries to block it. We both jump toward the net and smash into each other, but I get the ball across. The ball touches down. Our point.

"No way," Jerry yells.

"It was legit," Aria says. "Clear spike."

"She was all up in my face," Jerry says.

"I landed a spike. You *tried* to block it," I say.

"This is a no-contact sport," Jerry says. He sounds like a toddler.

"Jerry, come on. You bumped into each other. It happens," Enrico says from behind me. The ball has rolled to me. I pick it up.

"I didn't mean to push you," I say.

"But if I try to block you with...everything flopping around over there and touch you, I get slammed with sexual assault."

"You missed the block. You're blaming that on me?" I ask.

"If you weren't bouncing around all over the place, it would be easy to keep track of the ball."

"Don't be a jerk," Enrico says to his friend.

"Can we just play?" Ponytail says.

"Fine by me," I say. I hand her the ball for her serve.

"It's our serve," Jerry says. "Maybe you need to sit out," he tells me.

"No way." I don't care that much about volleyball or PE class, but no way am I going to let Jerry tell me what to do.

"Then keep your melons out of my face," Jerry says.

And his words are like a push in the back that sends me raging toward him. I shove him in the chest. He's not expecting it. He is tall and strong, but I throw him off-balance. He stumbles. Trips over one of his teammates. His sneakers squeak on the gym floor. He falls on his butt.

"Coach! Did you see that?" Jerry yells.

"What now?" Ms. Myers stops coaching a team across the gym. She marches over.

"She pushed me. Violently," Jerry says.

"He had it coming," I say. I know that won't help.

"Someone had to do it, Ms. Myers," Ponytail says.

"There's no violence in my class," Ms. Myers says.

"Then there shouldn't be any hate talk," I say.

"How about wearing a bra?" Jerry says.

"That's enough. Both of you to Principal Stall's office."

"Ms. Myers—" I begin, but she holds up a hand.

"To the office, Liv. We'll settle this."

That's what I'm afraid of. Settling this with Jerry and a male principal. I've been through this before with dress code. It won't end well.

Chapter Five

I can describe Mr. Stall's office with my eyes closed. There's a corner desk that wraps around his desk chair. There are pictures of two kids with missing teeth up on a shelf. Two framed drawings, one of a potato in a cowboy hat and another of a superhero with a dinosaur mask.

Ms. Myers walks us in. "These two got into a dispute in class yesterday. I thought it was over, but it continued today," she says. "I'll be in the gym." She closes the door.

"Sit," Principal Stall says. I'd rather stand, but I sit. "What happened?" He looks right at Jerry when he asks. Like I'm not even there.

"Today she pushed me. Yesterday she hit me in the balls. Sir."

Now Principal Stall turns to me.

"It wasn't on purpose," I say.

"You pushed him by accident?"

Crap. "No. The volleyball in his testicles yesterday was an accident."

"The push was intentional?" Principal Stall asks.

"He was being creepy. Making comments about my boobs."

The principal turns to Jerry again, like a curious dog watching a tennis match.

"What about her?" Jerry points at me. I want to rip his arm off, but I hold back.

"What about Liv?" the principal says. I get the up-and-down look from him too.

"She's not wearing a bra," Jerry says, pointing.

I cross my arms over my chest. I slouch in my chair. The bell rings, but Mr. Stall won't dismiss us until this is over.

Mr. Stall sits up straight, trying to hide his discomfort. "This is a problem?" Mr. Stall asks Jerry.

"It's distracting. Yesterday she couldn't serve. Today I couldn't block a spike. You know, with everything bouncing around, I didn't want to get accused of touching her," Jerry says.

"I see," Mr. Stall says.

I have to say something. But it can't be defensive. Or offensive. "Principal Stall?" I want my voice to be strong. But it's shaking.

"Yes, Liv?"

"I'm wearing the proper gym uniform."

"I can see that." Is he trying to see if Jerry is right?

"I'm following the rules," I say.

"Technically." He might as well say *yeah, right*.

Now I can't help being defensive. "What does that mean?"

"One moment, please." Mr. Stall stands and opens his door, pops his head out and waves someone in. Ms. Myers returns and stands in the corner. "Leave the door open, please, Ms. Myers. Liv, please stand," Mr. Stall says.

"Why?" I ask.

Ms. Myers tilts her head at me, which says, *Just do it.*

I stand. I keep my hands crossed over my chest.

"Would you please..." Mr. Stall lets his arms hang loose at his sides, meaning I should do the same. Ms. Myers nods. I let my arms fall. There's the up-and-down look again. I may as well be wearing my too-short top and my too-tight leggings. I got in trouble for those all of last year. A second later Mr. Stall sits back at his desk. “You should be wearing the proper undergarments, especially in physical education class,” he says.

Jerry sits tall in his chair.

Ms. Myers doesn’t say a word.

“Proper undergarments? You mean for Jerry, right? Like a cup? A jock strap?”

“I mean a brassiere, Liv.”

Ms. Myers finally speaks up. “Principal Stall, I don’t think—”

“Thank you, Ms. Myers, for your assistance. You may prepare for your next class.” She’s been dismissed.

“That’s it?” Jerry says. “She pushed me to the ground.”

"He was body-shaming me," I say. And without caring about the consequences, I add, "You both are."

Mr. Stall looks up at me as I stand. "That was not my intention, Liv. I am trying to give everyone the benefit of the doubt. You seem set on making that difficult. Last year, with all the dress-code violations, and now this."

"I'm complying with the dress code now," I say.

"It's a technicality, but the way you dress should not distract others in their learning. It has clearly caused a disruption. Twice. By just the second day of school."

"What about him? He can be rude and offensive to girls and that's okay?"

No response. I don't wait to be dismissed. I leave the office. Mia is waiting for me at my locker.

"What happened?" she asks. "You look ready to bite someone's head off."

"Teachers pick on girls for what we wear. The boys run around half naked, treat us like trash, and it's all good."

"What can we do?" Mia asks.

"Crush the patriarchy?" I say.

"So nothing," Mia says with a laugh.

"No, not nothing," I say. "I mean it. Let's actually do something this time."

Mia looks thoughtful. "Big ask," she says. "Where do we start? Should we make posters or something? Ask Ms. Myers to help?"

I scoff. "No. We start with the boys."

Chapter Six

I swagger into the gym, no bra under my sweatsuit. It's my best shot at looking confident. Jerry is beyond dumb. He's holding two basketballs up to his chest. He lifts one, then the other, like they're on a seesaw. I guess those are supposed to be my boobs. I zero in on him like a dart pointed at a bull's-eye.

I reach for his hands to lift the balls higher. He flinches and takes a step back. "I'm perkier," I say.

Enrico laughs, but Jerry doesn't. "You wish," Jerry says. He turns to his friends. I move closer and tap one ball out of his hand. It bounces to the floor. I catch, bounce and dribble it. I run up to the net, ready for a layup. I throw the ball. It hits the backboard and circles the rim. It doesn't go in the net. It bounces away from me. I turn to catch it, but Enrico is standing at the foul line with the ball in his hand.

"Want to play a game of twenty-one?" Enrico asks. He holds the ball out for me to take.

At the other end of the gym, Ms. Myers is untangling volleyball nets. Jerry volunteers to help her.

"Yeah," I say.

"You start," Enrico says.

"Sure. You saw my terrible layup so you figure you've got this?" I ask.

"Exactly." His smile is kind and inviting. I take the ball, bounce it and throw. I miss completely, and Enrico runs to catch it. He's at an easy angle, and he swishes the ball into the net. He walks to the foul line for his next shot.

"Feet apart. Like this," he says. "Bend your knees a little, but don't jump—that'll throw off your aim. Let the ball roll off your fingertips as you push it forward. Take your time." He throws and gets it in. "See? Like a pro."

"A pro? You being drafted into the NBA?" I ask teasingly.

"You never know. Here. You try." He hands over the ball again.

"But it's your turn," I say.

"I need to train you into a worthy opponent," he says, smiling.

"Is that a compliment or an insult?" I ask.

"One hundred percent a compliment," he says. "You're tough."

I curl my arms around the ball and hold it close. "You think I'm tough? How?" I ask.

"You don't take people's crap." Enrico gestures for me to advance to the foul line. I stand next to him.

"Why should I?" I ask.

He kicks at my feet to show me to separate them. "Exactly. Not everyone calls out people's dumb stuff. It's cool." He bends his knees. "Like this. Still facing the net." He positions himself for a shot. I imitate his movements with the ball in my hands.

"Cool? Really?" I say. I hesitate to ask my next question, but something tells me Enrico will be honest. "It's not...a turnoff?"

"Nah. Shows you're willing to say what's on your mind. No bull."

"No bull," I repeat. I shoot. It goes in. "Yes!"

Enrico holds both his hands above his head for a high five. My hands are sweaty. He lowers his hands and moves for a fist pump, but my arms are already out, so I end up slapping his fist. Awkward.

"Good job," he says.

"Now are you going to let me beat you at twenty-one?" I ask.

"You can try."

"Thanks. And thanks for not being a jerk. I mean, Jerry's your friend, right?" I ask.

"We play basketball together. Not really friends. But I'm sorry for how he spoke to you."

I appreciate Enrico's apology, but it shouldn't be coming from him. We start our game of twenty-one, and Enrico stops me to give me pointers and tips. It works. He wins. But he doesn't clobber me.

"I play on the boys' team, but I also referee the intramural team," he says.

"What's that?" I ask.

"Noncompetitive. All genders, all levels, mixed. We change up teams each week. It's a good way to learn and play without the pressure. You should join." A few beads of sweat have formed on his forehead. Something about knowing his sweat comes from playing with me has my heart pumping.

"You done showing off?" Jerry is behind me, talking to Enrico. "We could use some help with the nets," he says. He looks at me holding the basketball. "You finally learn some skills?" he says, looking at the ball I'm holding to my chest.

"Yeah. Learned not to take your nonsense. You were a real jerk yesterday. I apologized about the ball in your nuts, and you still complained to the principal. You can't talk to girls the way you do."

Without his other friends to back him up, Jerry looks like a deflated ball. His face is sour. "Okay. Fine. Sorry," he says.

"See, that wasn't so hard, was it?" I ask. I throw the ball to him, which he catches, and I walk off to help untangle the nets. It takes less than a minute and then I have one up and installed. "Let's go already," I say.

Enrico walks past me to his spot on the court. "Tough like that," he whispers.

I look over at Mia, who watches Enrico walk past her. *Nice*, she mouths to me.

Enrico is nice. And cute. And strong. And an ally.

Chapter Seven

With running around in the gym and the extra nervous sweating, I'm starving by lunchtime.

"You all right?" Mia asks, slowly opening up her own lunch. "I saw you talking to Jerry again."

"I got him to apologize," I say.

"Doesn't sound like him." Laughter and cheering come from the opposite end of the cafeteria as members of the senior girls' volleyball team walk past in their uniforms. Short shorts and tank tops. Jerry whistles. "That sounds like him." Mia points. "So gross."

One of the girls, Ilana, pushes through the group of boys. I think she's resisting throwing her spaghetti at Jerry. I would not have the same restraint. Ilana approaches the garbage can next to me. She throws away her leftovers. "No wonder you kicked him in the balls," she says to me. "Wish I could have seen it." She walks off with her friends.

"People know about that?" I ask Mia. "And I didn't *kick* him."

"You know about high school gossip, right? It's a thing," Mia says.

"It was an accident. Who said I kicked him?" I ask.

"Who knows. Maybe one of the volleyball girls?" Mia says.

I stop eating. My appetite is suddenly gone.

"Don't worry about it," Mia says. "The story makes you look great."

"Sure. Except everyone will know I don't wear a bra," I say.

"I hadn't thought about that," Mia says.

"I have to thank you, Liv." It's Jerry's nasal voice. He's behind me, and I do not want to turn to face him.

"What for?" Mia asks.

"Ilana never would have looked at me before all this," he says.

"Did you not see the look of disgust on her face?" Mia says, and I burst out laughing.

"Even bad publicity is good publicity," Jerry says.

"Ew," I answer.

"Jerry!" one of the boys from his table calls out to him, and he walks up to us. "You have to see this." He hands Jerry a sheet of paper with a bunch of signatures on it.

"This is perfect," Jerry says. He takes the boy's pen and signs his name on the sheet. I read the heading. *Free the Boobs. A petition to allow girls to go braless.* "See, Liv? I'm supporting you. Don't say I didn't try. Want to sign?"

I don't think about it. I whip my half-eaten sandwich in his face and march away. I hear Mia yell something at Jerry before she follows me down the hall. "Liv, wait!" she yells.

I can't stop. I run down the hall, straight out the back door. "Hang on." She catches up with me.

"I want to squeeze the brains out of his head," I say.

"Might struggle to find any. Not sure there are any brains in there," Mia says. "Like squeezing out the last of the toothpaste."

I can't help it. I laugh.

"In a zombie invasion, the monsters would walk right by Jerry. *No brains...no eat.*" Mia is walking around with her arms extended, dragging one foot. My laugh gets Mia going, and she stops to cross her legs.

"What's with the petition? I thought he was distracted by boobs," I say.

"Boys are weird. His friends were probably all like, *Bro, what do you mean, you want girls to wear bras? Imagine all of them, like, free and stuff. It would be awesome!*" She struts around talking in a deep voice. I laugh again, but then I remember how much I hate Jerry.

"How do I get back at him?" I ask.

"You don't," Mia says.

"I can't let him keep doing this," I say.

"No. You can't. We just have to do something better. Smarter."

"Like what?" I ask.

"Make a stand instead of getting revenge. I have an idea," Mia says.

Mia leads me into the art studio. "We have to come up with an advertisement for art class, right? So how about something like this?" She starts to sketch on a blank sheet.

"Hi, girls." Ms. Arturo, whom we call Ms. Art, comes over to us. "Working on your advertisement project?" She looks down at Mia's sketch. "Bras?"

"Sort of," Mia says. She continues sketching. "What do you think, Ms. Art?"

"Is this about what happened in gym class?" she asks me.

"The teachers know too?" I ask.

"Sorry. Word travels fast around here. But I'm all for this." She picks up Mia's sketch.

Several girls stand, backs to the viewer, in various types of uniforms. One clearly for soccer, with long socks. Another basketball, with a sleeveless pinny. Another volleyball, the girl in short shorts. Each girl holds up a bra. In the background spectators stand, hands raised or clapping, cheering the girls on.

"Something is missing," Ms. Art says.

"A slogan," I say.

"Do you have a way with words, Liv?" Ms. Art asks me.

"How about something to do with support?" I ask.

"Support girls without bras?" Mia suggests.

I cringe. "Nah. That's no good."

I remember Mia's joke about Jerry having no brains. "How about *With your support, who needs a bra? It's a No-BRAiner.*"

Ms. Art's eyebrows go up. "It's direct," she says. "I'd support that."

I smile. Wide. "Thanks," I say.

Mia and I spend the rest of the lunch hour drawing and coloring Mia's sketch onto a poster board. A few other girls in the art room check us out and offer to help us color it in. By the end of the lunch hour, we've created a clear, strong ad.

"Do you think we can put it up?" Mia asks Ms. Art.

"What else are advertisements for?" the teacher says. She pins it to the bulletin board outside the art studio. "It looks great."

"Do you think anyone will want to take it down?" I ask, thinking of Mr. Stall.

"Maybe," Ms. Art says. "Someone may try. There could be vandalism. Are you willing to take the chance?"

"Yes!" Mia and I say together.

I look at our poster again. "I just noticed something," I say, pointing to the girls on the poster. "The sports uniforms, the basketball pinny, the volleyball shorts..." I wait for Mia to catch on.

"Ha. They all violate the dress code." She gets it.

"Ironic?" I ask.

"Illogical," she says. "Makes the poster better."

I leave the art studio feeling empowered by Ms. Art's positive feedback. I don't even mind the problem-solving in math class. But near the end of the period, I imagine people like Jerry tearing down the poster. I'm afraid I've made a terrible mistake.

On my way to my locker, I pass the bulletin board.

My poster is still there.

Someone has added a sheet of paper next to it.

It's the petition. There are sixty-three names. Someone has crossed out Jerry's name near the top and in green ink written *Creep* above it.

The last name on the list is also written in green ink. Whoever put this up, it was to show their support of us, not of Jerry's stupid idea.

The last signature is messy, but it's clear enough to make out.

Enrico Delva

My heart is in my throat.

And I smile.

Chapter Eight

The next morning I'm sitting alone in Mr. Stall's office. The secretary says he'll be right over, but I'm missing art class, so I think he's taking his time on purpose.

Finally he walks in, buttoning up his blazer.

"Good morning, Liv," he says. He keeps the office door open.

"Why am I here, sir?"

"Ms. Arturo said you and Mia drew the poster. The one pinned up outside her studio."

He arranges some papers on his desk, then leans his elbows on it.

"It's for an art project," I say, already defensive.

"I understand that. However..." He clasps his hands together. "I'm afraid I had to take it down, along with this." He shows me the petition.

"I had nothing to do with that," I say. "My name isn't on it."

"I know. What about this?" He points to *Creep*.

"That wasn't me either. I wrote my name on my poster, if you want to compare handwriting," I say.

"I believe you," Mr. Stall says.

"So why am I here?" I ask again.

"Because your poster's intention is to challenge school rules."

"There are no rules that say I have to wear a bra. I checked."

"It goes without saying, Liv," the principal says.

"Who decided that? And why would they? Why is my body such a hot topic? The project was to create an ad. Something for or against a social issue," I say.

"Undergarments are hardly a social issue," Mr. Stall says.

"You just made them one by calling me out on it. And everyone knows about it. Bras are not the issue, but sexism is. Harassment. Body-shaming. I'm sorry, but I think you missed the point, Mr. Stall."

He tilts his head up and then back down to look at me. He stands. I stand too. "You are not dismissed," he says. He looks confused.

"I wasn't going to leave," I say.

"You may sit then." Mr. Stall gestures to my chair.

"I am comfortable standing if you are, Mr. Stall," I say. I can tell he doesn't know what to do next. We both stay where we are.

"Tomorrow is the school's open house," he says.

"I know."

"Parents will be visiting. Families. Artworks will be displayed for them to admire," he says.

"That's good," I say.

"Your poster will not be among them."

"Because it challenges the norm that girls should wear bras while doing sports?" I ask. "Even though their sports uniforms violate the dress code?"

His lips tighten. His neck is red. I feel heated too, but I am enjoying watching him get angry.

"I've tried to put everything aside from last year," he says. "Give you a fresh start. But it is early in the year to be inciting protest."

"Think of all the changes we've made in our society, Mr. Stall. Most of them started with a protest. A poster on a wall is as silent and peaceful as they come," I say.

"Is that a threat, Liv?" he asks.

"I don't know, Mr. Stall. But you shame me for what I wear. Or don't wear. What I look like.

And you don't let me express how I feel about it. Then you want to take down my artwork. But at least sixty-three other students agree with me. I don't think any of us will care that tomorrow is open house. But we do care about a standard that shames and sexualizes teenage girls."

"That is enough, I think, Liv. I have never openly shamed or sexualized any of my students," he says.

"Maybe not, Mr. Stall. But how would anyone know if I am or am not wearing a bra? If trying to figure that out is more important than me playing volleyball or attending my art class, I'm not the problem," I say. My voice isn't shaking. I sound calm. The way my mom does when she gets on my case about not doing chores. It drives me crazy when she doesn't yell at me. Now I understand why. Mr. Stall doesn't seem to like it either.

He looks relieved when there is a knock at the door. It's Ms. Myers.

"Yes, Ms. Myers?" Mr. Stall asks.

"I want to say, Mr. Stall, I was listening at the door."

"Oh?" He looks surprised. Then he looks like someone who is outnumbered.

"Liv is a smart girl. She is confident and sure of herself. We cannot punish her for that. She has been compliant, has listened to both of us, and has listened to her classmates judge her for something unrelated to her education. I think we should respect her privacy and her willingness to stand up for herself," Ms. Myers says.

"I see. And what of the boys in your class who came with concerns, Ms. Myers?" Mr. Stall asks.

"One boy, Mr. Stall. It was one boy. One, I might add, who started this petition to demean Liv. And her classmates turned it into an act of support for her choices. The adults should do the same. Liv? What class are you supposed to be in?" Ms. Myers asks me.

"Art class."

"May she return, Mr. Stall?" Ms. Myers asks.

"Mr. Stall, I'm not going to riot or stage a walk-out or anything like that. But I want to leave the poster up. Who will it hurt?" I ask.

Mr. Stall doesn't answer me. "Get back to class, Liv," is all he says.

Ms. Myers walks me to the art studio.

"I didn't do a great job of supporting you," she says.

"Are you kidding? He was speechless. That was perfect," I say. We reach the bulletin board. "It really is a great piece," Ms. Myers says. "You and Mia did a great job."

That's when it hits me. Mia's name is also on the poster. She did most of the work. But Mr. Stall only called me into his office. Mia pops her head out into the hall.

"Where were you?" she asks. She sees Ms. Myers. "Everything okay?"

I tell her where I was and what the principal said. "How come he didn't want to talk to me?" she asks.

"Exactly what I was thinking," I say.

"It's unfair on so many levels," Mia says.

“You’re right,” Ms. Myers says. “But I have a feeling the issue is at rest. Because Liv did a great job standing up for herself. And for all the girls.”

“But she didn’t have to do it alone,” Mia says. “That’s the point. She’s not alone.” Mia grasps my hand. I squeeze it gently.

“Thanks, Mia. Thanks, Ms. Myers.”

She nods and leaves as Mia and I enter the art studio.

“Enrico signed the petition. I saw it before Mr. Stall pulled it down,” Mia says.

Now I know my cheeks are flushed. And I know Mia can tell.

Chapter Nine

We help set up the studio for the open house. We fill the display cases with sculptures. Paintings are pinned to the wall.

"Liv," Ms. Art calls to me. "Your classmates prepared something for you." A collage of drawings is laid out on a table. There are different styles of art—graffiti, manga, cartoons, realistic portraits—and all are of girls, beside objects like books, paintbrushes, sneakers.

"What's this?" I ask.

"I asked the class to draw a girl—a smart girl, a happy girl, a passionate girl—alongside an object to represent their passion. We'll get your poster back and hang them together. What do you think?"

I love it. There is nothing to sexualize these girls. Some are wearing colorful clothing. Some are wearing tight clothes. Some have cleavage showing, but the emphasis is on them. The girls. Their style. Their objects. "It's perfect," I say. "But..."

"Don't worry. I'll keep it safe in the locked glass case down the hall. I'm the only one with the key."

"Great," I say. Mia and I start carefully picking up everyone's work and pinning the pieces onto the bulletin board in the case. Ms. Art locks it. The class steps out to admire our work.

The bell rings for recess, and Mia and I turn to collect our things from the art studio just as Enrico walks in.

"Hey," he says. His smile is bright. His brown hair is a bit frizzy, probably from the unexpected humidity today.

"Hi," I say. I rinse some paintbrushes.

"I saw your ad on the bulletin board. They took it down?" he asks.

"Ms. Art got it back. It's behind the glass case. You should check out the whole display."

"Pretty cool." He leans up against the sink, and I can smell sweat, but not the bad kind.

"What did you say to Principal Stall when he took it down?" Enrico asks. He helps me rinse the palettes.

"I may have, not in these exact words, suggested that the sixty-three people who signed the petition would possibly protest."

"Wow," he says. "Were you bluffing?" I dry while he washes.

"Definitely," I say.

"About the petition...I hope you know I signed it in support, not like Jerry."

"Oh, I know. Thanks," I say. I look at him. His dark eyes crinkle into a smile.

"I guess Jerry's idea backfired," Enrico says.

"What was his plan, anyway?" I ask.

"I think he wanted you to look dumb but

totally underestimated his own stupidity," he says. I laugh. "I was planning, for the open house tomorrow, to have the intramural basketball team play a game at lunch. So parents can see what we do in our free time. You could join us, if you're still interested," he says.

"Yes. Sounds fun," I say.

"And since tomorrow is Friday, I thought we could hang out after school," he says.

"Sure. What does the team usually do on a Friday?" I ask.

I place the palettes in the drawer. Mia and Ms. Art are clearing up the tables. Mia looks over at me. She makes a face. Then she asks Ms. Art another question.

"I meant us," Enrico says. "You and me. Hanging out. I mean, if you want to. No pressure."

"Right. Sorry," I say. *Oh, so awkward.* "Where do you like to hang?" I ask.

"How about Smitty's? All-day breakfast? Breakfast poutine! Nothing better. My treat," he says.

"I've never been to Smitty's," I say. Because I don't know how else to react to his intense excitement over breakfast poutine.

"All the more reason then," he says.

"Sounds great. Thanks." We leave the studio and walk by the display case.

"It's so simple. Perfect," he says.

"You think the parents will get it when they see it?" I ask.

"I don't know. Sometimes adults miss the point, but the drawings are amazing. It's a great showcase of the school's talent. Maybe I can add to it," Enrico says.

"What would you draw?" I ask.

"You. With breakfast poutine," he says, laughing.

"You think I'll like it that much?" I ask.

"It might be the best thing about our date," he says. I envy his dark skin because I know I'm blushing.

"I doubt it," I say.

Chapter Ten

The next day parents flood into the gym to watch our basketball game. Enrico pauses to set our positions. It feels good to be with a group of beginners. We are all learning. There is no pressure to be great. The parents cheer us on. They watch as Enrico talks another girl through her layup. She gets the ball in the net and we all cheer.

When the game is over, I head to the

locker room with the other girls. I don't bother hiding in the changing room. I'm able to pull off my gym T-shirt and pull on a clean one without anyone seeing anything.

"Good game," a girl says to me.

"You too," I say.

"I think what you said to Mr. Stall about not wearing bras was really cool, by the way," one girl says. She's younger than me. I don't even know her name.

"Yeah?" I say.

"I hate wearing them. Especially during sports. They're tight and make me sweat even more. So uncomfortable," she says.

"Comfort and feeling good. That's what should be important," I say.

"Thanks for saying that," the girl says. I don't ask how she knows what I said to Mr. Stall. It doesn't matter how.

I meet Enrico outside the gym.

"Great game," he says. "You learn quickly."

"Because I have a great coach," I say. "Want to check out the art display?"

"Yeah," he says.

As we approach, a group of parents is being guided around the studio by some volunteer students. Some are looking at the display case near the art studio.

"What do you think they see?" I ask Enrico.

We stop to listen in on their conversations. One woman in sports leggings and a hoodie with an oversized purse across her shoulder says, "It's about time."

"I don't get it," the man next to her says.

She gives him a side-eye so intense that I laugh. She notices us. Enrico and I duck into the art studio. "See? She got it," Enrico says.

"I hope she'll explain it," I say.

"We're still on for after school?" Enrico asks.

"Breakfast poutine awaits," I say.

When we leave the art studio, the woman with the large purse is, in fact, explaining the display to the man. And he is quiet. And listening. Nodding. Appreciating the drawings. "Okay," he says. "I get it."

I think we made them see.

There is more to us than what we wear.

"It's a no-BRAiner," the woman says. She emphasizes the *BRA* in the word.

"Huh," the man says. "That's smart."

I want to listen in a little more, but Enrico places his hand on the small of my back to lead me toward the door. "This okay?" he asks.

"Yeah." I slide my hand around his hip, and we set out to our next class.

Acknowledgments

Thank you to Gabrielle Prendergast at Orca for seeing the necessity of telling Liv's story and agreeing to work on this manuscript with me. Thank you to the editors at Orca for helping me find the right words to give Liv the confidence she deserves.

Thank you to the teachers and librarians who seek out books like this one to hook young striving readers.

I grew up around supportive women. They were the hand on my shoulder, the voices telling me I could do whatever I wanted if I worked hard enough. I observed as some struggled, yet thrived. I observed strength, and I took in all that I could. They are everywhere in my books. I hope they see themselves reflected here in a prism of color. Thank you for your constant support.

Maureen Marovitch, thank you for always saying yes to reading drafts and giving me honest feedback. I appreciate and value every word of it.

Sébastien Neveu, thank you for listening to me prattle on about books, even when we were like two ships passing in the night with little time to chat. You always let me have all the words. I'll never know anyone else with as much integrity and patience as you. You choose with kindness and do what is best for the children in your care. I love you.

I work with young people who have strong values and express them articulately and passionately when they know their adults are listening. Thank you to my students, who have spent their spare time sharing their insights about dress codes and body positivity. I will let you have all the words.

Raising a young girl to take a stand, take up the space she needs and make her voice heard takes grit, patience and a lot of explaining that sometimes things will be twice as hard for her because she is a girl. Éloïse, I hope this world is ready for you, my dear, because you are an elegant force. Raising two young men to understand how frustrating it is for girls to have to take a stand, make space and be loud just to be heard also takes grit, patience and explanation. Patrick and Dylan, I am proud of the young men you are becoming. This world needs you.

To my readers, thank you for trusting me enough to start and finish this book. I wrote it with you in mind, with admiration. All my gratitude to you for reading.

FIND YOUR NEXT

Poppy and her brother are home alone when a nearby wildfire heads straight for their farm. Can they get to safety with all the animals in tow?

Max uses AI to cheat on an essay and thinks all his problems are solved. But then the AI program starts blackmailing him...

THRILLING READ!

When teen vlogger Malika spends the night in the notoriously haunted Bhangarh Fort, her hope to record a viral video doesn't exactly go as planned.

Jesse doesn't have enough savings to buy a cool new pair of sneakers...until an older kid suggests robbing the local corner store. Will Jesse compromise his morals to fit in?

Lea Beddia is the author of books for young-adult striving readers. She is also a high school English teacher. Lea grew up in Montreal, where she had a hard time learning French, but with time, practice and the right books, she can now say she is bilingual (trilingual, if you include the Italian she grew up with). She loves gelato, zombies and stories that show young people they can be powerful. She lives in Joliette, Quebec, with her husband and three children.